LITTLE MISS SUNSHINE
keeps her smile

Original concept by Roger Hargreaves
Illustrated and written by Adam Hargreaves

World International

Little Miss Sunshine lives in Rise and Shine Cottage on the bank of a river.

And Little Miss Sunshine, as her name suggests, is a very happy person.

The sort of person who never gets in a bad mood.

The sort of person who is the exact opposite of somebody else who appears in this story.

That somebody is Mr Grumpy.

And Mr Grumpy, as his name suggests, is the grumpiest person in the world.

The sort of person who is always in a bad mood.

Everything annoys him.

Flowers growing in his garden. Sunny days ... and rainy days. But the thing that puts Mr Grumpy in the worst possible mood is seeing other people happy.

One morning Mr Grumpy met Little Miss Sunshine.

"Good morning Mr Grumpy," said Miss Sunshine cheerfully.

"There is nothing good about it," snapped Mr Grumpy.

"Humph," huffed Mr Grumpy, after Miss Sunshine had left. "That Miss Sunshine is always so abominably happy! Just for once I'd like to see her in a bad mood."

It was on his way home that Mr Grumpy thought of a plan. A plan to upset Little Miss Sunshine.

He raced home and made a list of all the things that were guaranteed to upset him.

It was a very long list!

"Now, there must be something here that will put Miss Sunshine in a bad mood," he said to himself.

Mr Grumpy was not a very nice man!

The first thing Mr Grumpy had written on his list was, 'waiting for buses'.

So the next day Mr Grumpy opened a gate and let all Farmer Field's sheep out into the lane! And the bus was delayed for hours and hours while all the sheep were rounded up.

Mr Grumpy ran round to the bus stop.

"Tee hee," he chuckled nastily, "I can't wait to see how upset Miss Sunshine is."

But Little Miss Sunshine was not upset.

In fact she was not there.

It was such a nice day she had decided to walk into town.

"Bother!" said Mr Grumpy.

The next day Mr Grumpy looked at the second thing on the list.

"Losing," he read out loud.

So that evening he invited Miss Sunshine round to his house to play cards and ... he cheated!

But Little Miss Sunshine being the happy-go-lucky person she is did not mind losing.

Mr Grumpy won every game they played.

"Oh, well played Mr Grumpy," she said at the end of the evening.

"Bother, bother," said Mr Grumpy after she had left.

Mr Grumpy read down his list again.

Number three said, 'getting caught in the rain'.

Mr Grumpy filled up his watering can and, using his ladder, climbed a tree just outside Miss Sunshine's house.

And there he waited until Miss Sunshine came out for her walk.

But Little Miss Sunshine saw the ladder.

"What a silly place to leave a ladder," she said to herself, and walked round the other side of the tree and put the ladder away.

"Bother, bother, bother," muttered Mr Grumpy, who ended up stuck in the tree all night.

Well, nearly all night. Just before sunrise he fell asleep ... and fell out of the tree!

The fourth thing on Mr Grumpy's list was 'queues'.

Mr Grumpy waited until Little Miss Sunshine went shopping and then he rushed ahead of her to the greengrocer's. Where he started an argument with Mrs Pod about the quality of her peas.

As he argued a queue began to form behind him and when he glanced back he saw Miss Sunshine standing at the back of the queue.

He smiled to himself and carried on arguing until he felt sure she must be fed up of waiting.

But when he turned round the queue had disappeared and when he went outside he found everyone in the queue happily chatting with Little Miss Sunshine.

"Double bother, bother!"

Mr Grumpy was furious.

But then he met Mr Nosey and had another thoroughly nasty idea.

"Do you know," said Mr Grumpy, "what Little Miss Sunshine calls Miss Bossy behind her back. She calls her knobbly knees!"

Mr Grumpy's thoroughly nasty idea was to start a rumour that would get Little Miss Sunshine into trouble.

And the rumour spread.

Mr Nosey told Little Miss Star who told Mr Uppity who told Little Miss Splendid who told ... Mr Muddle ... who told Little Miss Bossy.

" ... and Little Miss Sunshine said that Mr Grumpy calls you knobbly knees," said Mr Muddle.

"Does he now!" said Miss Bossy grimly, and marched straight round to Mr Grumpy's house and biffed him on the nose!

It was a very sorry looking Mr Grumpy that Little Miss Sunshine met outside her house the next day.

Miss Sunshine invited him in for breakfast to cheer him up and cooked him fried eggs.

Sunny side up of course!

And did she manage to cheer up Mr Grumpy?

Of course not!

No more than Mr Grumpy can upset Little Miss Sunshine!

3 Great Offers For Mr Men Fans

1 FREE Door Hangers and Posters

In every Mr Men and Little Miss Book like this one you will find a special token. Collect 6 and we will send you either a brilliant Mr. Men or Little Miss poster and a Mr Men or Little Miss double sided, full colour, bedroom door hanger. Apply using the coupon overleaf, enclosing six tokens and a 50p coin for your choice of two items.

Egmont World tokens can be used towards any other Egmont World / World International token scheme promotions., in early learning and story / activity books.

Posters: Tick your preferred choice of either Mr Men ☐ or Little Miss ☐

Door Hangers: Choose from: Mr. Nosey & Mr Muddle ☐, Mr Greedy & Mr Lazy ☐, Mr Tickle & Mr Grumpy ☐, Mr Slow & Mr Busy ☐, Mr Messy & Mr Quiet ☐, Mr Perfect & Mr Forgetful ☐, Little Miss Fun & Little Miss Late ☐, Little Miss Helpful & Little Miss Tidy ☐, Little Miss Busy & Little Miss Brainy ☐, Little Miss Star & Little Miss Fun ☐. (Please tick)

2 Mr Men Library Boxes

Keep your growing collection of Mr Men and Little Miss books in these superb library boxes. With an integral carrying handle and stay-closed fastener, these full colour, plastic boxes are fantastic. They are just £5.49 each including postage. Order overleaf.

3 Join The Club

To join the fantastic Mr Men & Little Miss Club, check out the page overleaf NOW!

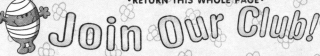

Join Our Club!

MR MEN & Little Miss CLUB

When you become a member of the fantastic Mr Men and Little Miss Club you'll receive a personal letter from Mr Happy and Little Miss Giggles, a club badge with your name, and a superb Welcome Pack (pictured below right).

You'll also get birthday and Christmas cards from the Mr Men and Little Misses, 2 newsletters crammed with special offers, privileges and news, and a copy of the 12 page Mr Men catalogue which includes great party ideas.

If it were on sale in the shops, the Welcome Pack alone might cost around £13. But a year's membership is just £9.99 (plus 73p) with a 14 day money-back guarantee if you are not delighted!

HOW TO APPLY To apply for any of these three great offers, ask an adult to complete the coupon below and send it with appropriate payment and tokens (where required) to: Mr Men Offers, PO Box 7, Manchester M19 2HD. Credit card orders for Club membership ONLY by telephone, please call: 01403 242727.

To be completed by an adult

❑ **1.** Please send a poster and door hanger as selected overleaf. I enclose six tokens and a 50p coin for post (coin not required if you are also taking up 2. or 3. below).

❑ **2.** Please send __ Mr Men Library case(s) and __ Little Miss Library case(s) at £5.49 each.

❑ **3.** Please enrol the following in the Mr Men & Little Miss Club at £10.72 (inc postage)

Fan's Name:_____Fan's Address:_____

_____

_____Post Code:_____Date of birth:___/___/___

Your Name:_____Your Address:_____

_____

Post Code:_____Name of parent or guardian (if not you):_____

Total amount due: £_____ (£5.49 per Library Case, £10.72 per Club membership)

❑ I enclose a cheque or postal order payable to Egmont World Limited.

❑ Please charge my MasterCard / Visa account.

Card number: | | | | | | | | | | | | | | | | |

Expiry Date: _____/_____   Signature: _____

Data Protection Act: If you do **not** wish to receive other family offers from us or companies we recommend, please tick this box ❑. Offer applies to UK only